MW00653684

FROZEN FUN

Cover Illustration by Margarita Sikorskaia

Softcover ISBN 13: 978-1-7346743-8-5
Hardcover ISBN 13: 978-1-7346743-7-8

Printed in the United States of America

Cover and interior design by James Monroe Design, LLC.

Lucky Luke, LLC.
4335 Matthew Court
Eagan, Minnesota 55123

www.KevinLovegreen.com
Quantity discounts available!

Chapter 1

I wake up, and it takes me only a second to remember where I am. A giant half-moon smile raises my cheeks. I rise and look out the little window behind me. The sun isn't up, but the calm blue glow of a cold February morning says it's close.

I look over at my older sister, Crystal, lying on the little bed next to me. She isn't moving, still dead asleep. Typical for a fourteen-year-old girl.

I slide out of my sleeping bag and shuffle across the wooden floor to the old black cast-iron stove. The big logs Dad stuffed in last night are still kicking out heat. I warm my hands for a moment.

I scoot over and peek out into the living room. The fireplace out there is almost done. I figure I better add some more wood if the cabin's going to stay warm. Especially in the middle of winter here in Minnesota.

I step through the doorway into the living room, and the cool air sends a chill up my back. I look out the window at the big round thermostat attached to the old oak tree.

Zero.

I shiver, imagining how cold it must feel out there. It doesn't seem to bother the oak tree, though.

I add a few split pieces of red pine to the fireplace. I shut the mesh grate and take a big, deep breath to blow on the orange embers. Like magic, a flame appears. I smile and give the fire a nod of thanks for being so cooperative.

I pull a chair next to the fireplace and look outside. The long row of windows provides a nice view. Like a king entering the celebration, the sun is emerging across the frozen lake covered in deep snow.

In fact, if you didn't already know there was a lake out there, you might mistake it for a big meadow. In wintertime, everything sort of looks the same when it's blanketed by a bunch of snow.

I'm Luke, and this is one of my favorite places in the world—my grandparents' cabin in northern Minnesota. I love hunting, fishing, and all outdoor stuff. And up here, we get to do it all. Even snowmobiling and ice fishing!

Grandma and Bapoe didn't come up this weekend, so it's only our family. Mom, Dad, and Crystal are still sleeping. We arrived late last night because of the five-hour drive.

A chickadee lands on the wooden bird feeder that stands about five steps from the windows. Then a yellow-and-black bird lands next to the chickadee. Bapoe told me those colorful birds are called evening grosbeaks.

I look up in the giant pine tree that watches over the cabin and the bird feeder. I see a bunch more grosbeaks sitting on the branches. Five of them fly to the feeder. Two perch on each side. One grosbeak can't find a spot, so it lands on top, which is full of snow.

This is the only place I see these birds. They must love it up here in the north country.

Suddenly a big bossy blue jay crashes the party and scares the grosbeaks all back to the safety of the giant pine branches. Then the blue jay digs into the birdseed like he's looking for one specific piece on the bottom. Seeds fly out and disappear into the deep snow.

Snacks for a tunneling mouse, I guess!

Then I catch some movement to my right. Two white-tailed deer appear out of the woods. It's a big doe—the mama deer—and her fawn.

I keep perfectly still. They will see me through the windows if I move.

The mom takes her time and cautiously moves to the bird feeder. She sticks her nose down into the snow. Then she uses her right front hoof to scratch open a spot. From all the chewing she's doing, it looks as though she found the seeds the blue jay scattered. I guess that mouse will have to share.

I stay still and feel the wonderful heat from the fireplace. I can't help but smile again. This place is so cool.

I hear the kitchen floor creaking. Someone else must be up. I keep watching the doe to see how she reacts to the sound and movement.

Her head turns left, and her ears swivel and cup toward the window. She clearly hears or sees someone.

"You have a visitor, I see," a voice behind me says. It's Dad.

"Yep," I reply. "And she sees you."

The deer turns slowly around and high-steps through the snow back into the woods. Her little one is right behind her.

"Good morning, Luke," Dad says. "Looks like a perfect day to go ice fishing."

My tired eyes don't need any help waking up now. I'm fired up. I love ice fishing! And the best ice fishing in the world is up here at the cabin.

"Ice fishing would be awesome!" With a beaming smile, I look at Dad.

"Great! I'm thinking Boney's Lake," Dad says.

My eyes get even wider. Boney's Lake is one of my favorite places to fish. We call it Boney's Lake because a guy named Mr. Boney used to live there way before I was born.

The lake is small, tucked back in the woods, and loaded with monster bass, giant sunfish, and huge northern pike. I love fishing the lake our cabin is on, but we catch way more fish through the ice on Boney's. And we get to ride our snowmobiles on the way there. A total bonus!

Dad's eyes light up too. "It's a deal, then. We'll get going after breakfast."

He gazes at the snow-covered lake for a moment. Then he turns and gives me a special wink.

"There's some fresh powder out there," he says. "I think it needs some tracks in it. Maybe you'll have time to get in a few hot laps on your snowmobile before we head out for Boney's."

"Sweet!" I exclaim.

That's the green light to take my snowmobile out for some fun. Like a jackrabbit, I spring to life and race for my gear. I high-five Dad as I rush by.

"Hold your horses," Mom says. She walks out of the bedroom. "Let's get some food in you before you go outside."

And just like that, I have pancakes on my mind.

This is gonna be a great day!

Chapter 2

Breakfast is a feast: fluffy pancakes, crispy bacon, sweet watermelon chunks, and tasty orange juice. As delicious as it is, we're all excited to get to Boney's!

After cleaning up, Crystal and I fly over to our duffel bags. In a flash, I'm snuggled inside all my winter gear and ready to ride.

I beat Crystal in our race to get ready, so I'm the first out the front door. I slowly tread across the short wooden deck.

It creaks with each step. It sounds like I'm breaking the cold out of it.

I carefully walk down the four icy steps. When I hit the crusty snow at the bottom, my boots crunch like I'm stepping on Styrofoam.

There it is. My trusty snowmobile sits next to the trailer. Through the frost, I see "Lucky Luke" written on the hood. Crystal's name is written on her sled too. In purple, of course.

Dad and Mom gave us the snow-mobiles for Christmas this year. They're by far the greatest Christmas gifts we've ever received. Even if the sleds aren't new, they're ours. We love riding them!

Dad comes outside and heads to the garage. Next, Mom and Crystal come out, all bundled up. They're carrying a big white cooler together.

I run over to help. Once they're down the steps, I take over for Mom. The cooler isn't that heavy, but it's big. Crystal and I carry it and carefully set it next to the yellow sleigh.

"You guys go make some tracks on the lake. Dad and I will load up the sleigh," Mom says.

With a whoop, we both run to our sleds.

Starting a snowmobile isn't as simple as starting a car. It's more like starting a lawnmower. To get the engine going, you have to yank a pull cord. And sometimes it takes more than one yank.

So, I turn the key on, push the choke up, and grab the pull cord with both hands.

Using all my might, I pull. It's like pulling a frozen rope.

It's cold out!

I let the line go back in. Next, I brace my right foot on the edge of the snowmobile and pull the cord again. A little easier this time, but still the engine doesn't fire. I let the line back in and pull again with a grunt, letting it know I mean business.

Nothing!

I look over at Crystal. She isn't having any luck starting hers either. The sleds clearly don't like this cold.

I pull again—and again and again. I'm not giving up. This engine *will* start. I'm determined to make the first tracks on the lake.

I stop pulling to catch my breath. Sweat is running down my back. Again, I grab the cord with both hands and give it everything I've got.

The engine lets out one pop.

"Yes!" I shout.

That's the hope I need. I let the line in and pull again with all my might.

Pop, pop!

Now I'm energized. I pull again and again. The engine sounds like it wants to start. I pull harder and harder.

Finally, just when I'm almost out of steam, the engine putters a breath of smoke. I pull one more time. The putter turns into a rumble.

I quickly grab the gas throttle and give it a push. Not all the way, just a little. I've watched Dad do this a hundred times. This time, I'm going to make it happen.

I'm breathing heavy. Steam is coming out of my mouth like I'm a dragon. I pull off my helmet to let the heat out. The cold air feels good on my hot head. Smoke billows from my cold snowmobile like fog filling a swamp.

Meanwhile, Crystal gives up on starting her sled. She heads to the garage to get Dad for help.

I'm even more determined now to get my sled going. I play the throttle, warming up the engine. The black-and-dark-blue hood of my Polaris snowmobile vibrates. It's finally awake! With each little push of the throttle, it revs powerfully.

I slide my helmet back over my red hair and buckle the chin strap. I hop on the snowmobile like it's a horse and take hold of the handle grips. It's warmed up and ready to go.

I give more gas, and the track spins and shoots the sled forward. I turn in the driveway and face the lake.

The next challenge is in front of me. The only thing keeping me from the fresh powder on the lake is a huge snowbank. Dad made it from plowing the driveway last night. It's taller than I am!

Staring the snowbank down, I take off. I hit the bank, going right up it like a ramp. I bend my knees to take the shock. With just the right push of the throttle, I launch over the bank. My skis lead the way through the air. Then I land softly in the deep snow on the other side.

Awesome!

Now I'm floating through the deep-powder snow. I go over the deer tracks, past the bird feeder, and down the big hill to the waiting lake. I level out when I shoot onto the lake. Then I lean into a right turn to follow the shoreline.

The sun is shining, and the pure white snow is sparkling. I'm flying across the lake, weaving back and forth on the powder. I bank to the left and keep following the shoreline around the lake.

When I make a full lap, I don't stop. Like I'm racing against myself, I start another lap on the small lake.

As I'm cruising, a thought comes to me. This lake is full of largemouth bass. I love catching bass. In the summer, you can't keep me off the lake. Now all those fish are tucked under the thick layer of ice.

Do they look up when I drive over them? Or do they shoot off and hide? That's something I've never thought about before!

Deep in thought, I look over and see another snowmobile. It's Crystal. Her purple helmet is easy to spot. I turn and cross the middle of the lake in her direction.

When I get close, Crystal gives me a thumbs-up.

I know what that means. The race is on!

She takes off down the shoreline. I squeeze the throttle and spin the track. It takes me halfway around the lake to finally get behind her. When we reach our cabin's shoreline, I pass her on the lake side.

With me in the lead, we race around for another lap.

When we near the cabin the second time, I turn right and fly up the big hill. Past the bird feeder, up and over the big snowbank, and back to the plowed driveway.

What a rush!

Crystal comes to a skidding halt next to me and kills her engine.

"How was your ride, kids?" Mom asks.

"Awesome! The snow is perfect," Crystal says.

"Yep," I agree.

Dad and Mom have the old yellow sleigh attached to their snowmobile. The sleigh is packed with all the ice fishing stuff. I see the red auger for drilling holes, four little fishing rods all wrapped up with fishing line, the orange tip-up, the white foam minnow bucket, a five-gallon bucket, and the green tackle box, all tucked behind the big white cooler. It looks like we're set.

"Let's get this show on the road!" Dad says.

With one mighty pull, Dad fires up his sled. Mom hops on behind him and wraps her arms around him tight. Dad turns the snowmobile and heads up over the snowbank toward the lake. The sleigh follows behind.

An uneasy feeling overcomes me as the sleigh climbs up the steep bank. As the sleigh nears the top, the white cooler and all the gear behind it slide to the back. But then once the sleigh makes it to the top and starts down on the other side, everything quickly rushes forward. The cooler and half the gear go flying out!

Crystal and I look at each other and shake our heads. What was Dad thinking?

Dad stops the snowmobile and looks back. "Oops," is all he says.

All we can do is laugh!

Crystal and I run over and help Dad load everything back into the sleigh. We are really lucky the minnow bucket didn't break open. Water and live minnows would have been everywhere.

With the gear secured in place, we finally head out. We follow Dad and Mom down the big hill toward the lake. I'm in the back to keep an eye on everything.

Dad stays in the fresh tracks Crystal and I made. Meanwhile, she and I make new tracks, floating in the fresh powder.

We follow Dad to the end of the lake. At the shoreline, he drives up the bank and joins the unplowed state road.

I know this road well because we grouse hunt down it every fall. It weaves through a big forest. The oaks and the white poplar trees are leafless, but the pine trees don't seem to care that it's winter. Their green needles still glow.

Now we're cutting our own tracks— no one else has been around here lately. The journey continues through the state land.

Dad leads the way. He's been coming up here for most of his life, so he knows all the trails like the back of his hand. I keep a safe distance back and watch Crystal as we cruise along.

After about twenty minutes, there it is.

The magical lake is in sight!

Chapter 3

I watch Dad go down the steep bank to get to the lake. Thankfully, nothing falls out of the sleigh this time.

I follow Crystal down and then shoot out past her onto the untouched snow. I race around the little lake, which doesn't take me long.

The only thing I see on the whole lake is a black fish house. It's just a big square plywood box that sits out there peacefully like it's the only little house on earth.

The fish house is Steve's. He's a senior in high school who lives near here. Our families have known each other for years. My grandpa and his grandpa were friends. That's how we ended up having a cabin way up north.

Steve is super cool and fun to hang out with. He traps, hunts, and knows all the best fishing spots up here. Each time we see him, he has a crazy story to tell—like the time he ran into six black bears when he was walking through a cornfield to go bow hunting for deer. Or the time he trapped a giant beaver, and it took him and a friend twenty minutes to drag it up a bank. I love his stories!

Every time we come to Boney's to ice fish, that black house is here. I've never been inside it, but I can only imagine how many fish Steve has caught in there.

I head back to help Dad, Mom, and Crystal set up. It's beautiful out—not a cloud in the pure-blue sky. The temperature has warmed up and feels good now. The best part is, if there were a flag around, it would be hanging straight down. There isn't a trace of wind.

Dad unloads the sleigh and sets everything in the snow.

"Luke, take my snowmobile and load up the sleigh with wood for a fire," he says.

Crystal and I look at each other, both a little shocked. This is the first time Dad has let me drive his big sled."On it!" I say.

I play it cool. I pull on my helmet, walk over to Dad's sled, and grab the pull cord. I give it a pull with all my might. To my surprise, it fires right up.

I look over to see if Dad noticed. He did. He smiles and gives me a thumbs-up.

Then I look at Crystal and give her a confident nod. She smirks and shakes her head. I'm not sure she thinks I'm as cool as I feel.

The engine rumbles with power. I can sense it through my whole body. I get on and try to ease the snowmobile forward. When I give it more gas, it shoots forward. Like a wild animal, it roars with strength. This snowmobile is amazing! It's like a team of horses ready to explode into a full gallop.

I let off quickly. There is so much power when I hit the throttle—I have to admit it's a little frightening.

I continue forward but take it easy across the lake. I don't want to ruin my chances of driving Dad's snowmobile again.

At the shore, I get to work gathering wood. I find a bunch of dead branches and load them into the sleigh. Then I head back to our fishing spot. We'll have a fire going in no time.

When I reach Dad, he already has two holes drilled into the ice. The thing about ice fishing is that you can't just throw your line out! You first have to cut through the ice in order to reach the water below.

To do that, you use a special drilling tool called an auger. Some augers run on gas or batteries. Ours runs on good old-fashioned muscle!

"Can I drill my own hole?" I ask.

Dad gives me the red auger with the black handle.

"Be my guest," he says.

I hunt around for a spot that feels just right.

"How deep do you think it is here?" I ask Dad. He knows this lake well.

"You're at about eight feet, I would guess," Dad says.

I figure that's perfect. I clear off the snow and set the blade on the ice. Then I push down and start cranking the handle. The corkscrew drill begins spinning.

The blade scratches at the ice and digs in, just like a bear clawing to get to a frozen fish. With each full turn, it digs into the ice about half an inch. I keep turning and turning, and it keeps cutting and cutting.

After a while, my arms feel like noodles, so I stop for a break. This is tough!

I'm breathing hard, but the clean cool air brings my strength back. I'm determined to get through this thick ice. There are fish down there that I'm going to catch!

I start again. The drill is now out of sight, deep in the ice. I keep cranking the handle and get into a steady rhythm. As I concentrate on the spinning drill, I'm reminded of Grandma's mixer making cookie dough. My mind wanders for a bit—I can almost smell Grandma's amazing chocolate chip cookies as I picture them coming out of the oven. Grandma makes the best cookies!

But then the drill catches on the ice, and I snap back to reality. I have to focus. That water is down there somewhere, and I have to reach it.

I pause, grit my teeth, and give it all I've got for a few spins. Finally, the drill busts through.

Victory at last!

I hold on tight to the handle as water rushes up the hole. I don't want to lose the drill to the bottom of the lake. I slide my feet back, keeping clear of the water spilling onto the ice.

Now it's time to flush the hole. I push the drill down deep and then quickly pull it out. This makes water surge up, clearing all the ice chips from the hole. Dad taught me this trick, and it works great.

Using my right boot, I scrape the pile of ice down smooth. I flush the hole one more time, which seems to complete the job.

I nod at the clear water, giving it my approval. "There we go!" I say triumphantly.

I look around for approval, but nobody heard me. They're all busy with their own projects.

It doesn't matter. It's time for fishing!

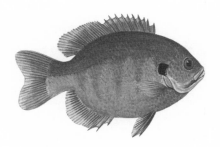

Chapter 4

Now that I'm done drilling my hole, I notice that Mom has a fire blazing.

"Nice fire, Mom. You rock!" I comment.

"Thanks," she says.

I grab my sweet little green fishing rod and a small container of wax worms. This rod has helped me catch a bunch of fish, and today should be no different.

Back at my hole, I carefully hook on a wax worm. I'm not sure what a wax worm really is, but I know it's not made out of wax. It's a real, live, white wiggly thing. I can't believe Crystal plays with them. Each time we go ice fishing, she puts a couple in her hand and lets them crawl around. She's so weird.

I look over and see Crystal and Dad setting up. Their holes are right next to each other.

"Are you guys ready? I'm all set!" I yell. I can be as loud as I want out here— there isn't anyone around for miles.

"Almost," Crystal says. "Give us one second."

Dad and Crystal finally get their wax worms hooked on.

"Ready!" Crystal raises her fishing rod like a warrior ready for a battle charge.

"Let's see who can catch the first fish. Fish on!" Dad commands.

Here we go!

I open the bail of my little black reel, which lets the line spool out. The tiny green jig with the wax worm dangling from its hook drops down the hole. When I feel like the jig is about six feet below the ice, I close the bail, and the line goes tight. I slowly jerk the rod up and down to give the bait some action. This is called jigging.

I hold my rod lightly and stare at the hole, waiting to sense any little bite. I feel like an Alaskan grizzly bear watching intently for the first salmon to swim upstream. I keep jigging and hoping, but nothing happens for a while.

"Come on, where are they?" I say. I look over at Dad, who smiles back.

"Patience, Luke. Good things come to those who wait," he says, knowing good and well neither of us has very good patience. I stare at my hole with more intensity. I know the fish are down there, so I decide to take a peek.

I get on my knees and put my face right into my hole. Using my hands to block the sunlight, I'm now looking at a whole other world down there. The water is crystal clear, and I can see all the way to the bottom.

There are brown weeds and big clumps of stuff that look like giant brown blobs on the lake bottom. We always see them when we're fishing in the summer. It's just how this lake is—I've never seen these clumps in any other lake.

Suddenly I feel a cold, wet sensation on my nose. I lean back in surprise.

Whoops! I was leaning so far down that my nose touched the water. I laugh at myself as some droplets fall off the end of my nose. Sometimes I get so focused on what I'm doing that things like this happen. I forget about everything else.

I put my head back down, making sure I don't get so close to the water this time. I can just make out my green jig down there. I strain to see more, but I'm limited to my little peek hole.

Then a small sunfish swims into view. It goes straight to my jig and takes a poke at my wax worm.

"Get out of here, little guy. I want something bigger than you."

On cue, three giant sunfish swim into the circle. That's what we're looking for!

I pull my head out and enter back into the snowy world. The sun is bright, and my eyes know it. I have to squint until my vision gets used to the light.

I begin jigging again. I bounce my rod tip up and down, hoping to entice the big sunnies to bite. I feel a little nibble. I stop jigging and let the tip of the rod slowly drop down. That lets my jig fall and usually causes a fish to bite. It thinks its snack is dropping to the bottom.

My line twitches again—I think one of the fish is taking the bait.

Bam!

I set the hook by pulling up. The unmistakable tug at the other end of the line confirms my feeling. The fight is on!

"Oh baby, I got one!" I yell.

I pull and reel, but the sunfish wants nothing to do with coming up to my hole. He spins in circles and gives it everything he has. I fight him until he finally starts calming down. I pull him up through the hole and raise him high in victory.

"First fish!" I declare.

I show him to Crystal, Dad, and Mom. My rod is bent over—he's a big one!

"Good job, Luke," Mom calls from the fire.

I take a better look at my catch. This sunny is huge. The sunfish in this lake can be giants—and I mean *giants*. This one is way bigger than my open right hand. I pop the hook out of his mouth, then run over and drop him in the white five-gallon bucket.

"That's one for dinner!" I smile proudly.

I race back to my hole. I can't wait to see how many more fish I can catch. But before I even get my line back into the water, Crystal is hooting. She's got one on!

I watch her pull a giant sunfish out. The smile on her face is priceless. Dad and Crystal high-five, and Dad unhooks the fish and plops it into the bucket.

"Good job, Crystal!" I yell. "Your turn, Dad," I say, egging him on. "Come on— let's see what you got!"

Dad just gives me a thumbs-up and a wink.

The game is on!

Chapter 5

And just like that, the game really *is* on. The fish must have realized food is down there, because they are striking like crazy. They're clearly hungry. One after another, the giant sunfish gulp up our wax worms.

For an hour, we hoot and holler and pull them in left and right. After we put ten in the bucket for dinner, we start tossing the rest back in the lake. It happens so fast that there's no way to keep count.

Dad taught us to keep only enough to eat and then have fun throwing the rest back. He says catching and releasing fish is a good way to keep lakes healthy. Even though I love eating fish, I also feel good throwing them back and giving them another chance.

From all the smiling, laughing, and hooting, I can tell we're all having fun. I'm sure the animals watching from the woods are wondering what's going on.

Before long, my stomach rumbles.

"Is it lunchtime yet?" I yell. I unhook another fat sunny from my jig and slide it back down the hole.

"Sounds good to me," Dad says.

I reel in my line and leave my rod next to the hole. Dad goes over to our pile of stuff in the snow and grabs the tip-up.

"Why don't you set this up before we eat," Dad says to me.

I had forgotten about the tip-up. It's pretty cool. It allows you to fish hands-free—and that comes in handy at lunchtime!

The tip-up has a big spool of line and a one-foot-tall orange flag attached to a thin wire rod. The tip-up also has a horizontal bar that reaches across the hole so it can't fall in. You drop the bait down and cock the flag, and when a fish bites and pulls the line out, the flag pops up.

I take off my right glove and grab a big lively sucker minnow from the minnow bucket. I tromp back to my hole and hook the minnow through the top of its back, near its tail. This will allow it to swim and won't kill it.

I ease the minnow down the hole and let out some line. After cocking the flag, I head to the fire.

"Well, let's see if something big wants to eat today," Dad says with wild eyes.

I can't stop looking over at the flag. There are some huge northern pike in this lake, and pulling them up through the ice is awesome. How did I forgot to drill another hole for the tip-up when we first got here?

By this point, Mom's fire is big and crackling with energy. Crystal and I run to the shore and find four perfect cooking sticks. Back at the fire, Dad gives me his little brown buck knife. I carve the end of each stick into a perfectly smooth point ready to stick a hot dog.

"They're ready!" I say. "Here you go, Crystal. Dad and Mom, do you want me to cook yours?"

"That would be nice. Thank you," Mom responds.

"I'll cook my own. Thanks for offering, Luke," Dad says.

I slide two hot dogs onto my stick and find a perfect spot on the side of the fire. I plop down and sit cross-legged. Not easy to do with my snowmobile bibs on, but I manage.

I slowly rotate the hot dogs. I want to make sure Mom's is perfect. She likes her hot dogs cooked well and brown all the way around.

I stare at the fire as the hot dogs roast. The glowing embers seem alive and are kicking out the perfect heat. The hot dogs start to sweat and bubble, and then one of them lets out a hissing sound. *Psssss*.

"I think it's whispering to you, Luke. It's letting you know it's almost done," Crystal says, giggling.

Now the hot dogs are perfectly brown. I pull them out of the fire and walk over to Mom. She already has hot dog buns popped open and ready on a paper plate. I slide the first hot dog onto a bun and hand it to her. Then I slide the second one onto another bun for myself. Mom reaches over and squeezes a perfect zigzag line of cherry-red ketchup on top of mine.

"Thank you, Mom," I say.

"Thank you, Chef Luke. Mine looks perfect."

With my mouth watering, I take a big bite. Instantly, I realize I shouldn't have. It's boiling hot! But there's no way I'm going to spit it out.

"Hi-ya-ya!" I exclaim, breathing in cool air and trying to put out the fire in my mouth. I carefully shift the food around, not letting it sit in one spot for too long. After a couple of seconds of quick mouth gymnastics, I chew and swallow.

"Whoa, that was hot," I shout, shaking my head.

"I would say that was very entertaining. Please do it again," Crystal jokes.

By the time I take a second bite, the cold winter air has cooled the hot dog to the perfect temperature. I gobble down the rest without incident. Then I grab another hot dog out of the pack and head back to the fire to start cooking again. There is something magical about being outside on a frozen lake and eating hot dogs from a fire. They taste amazing!

Suddenly, something causes all of us to turn our heads at the same time. We can hear a snowmobile growling in the distance, breaking the silence of this peaceful lake. We listen for a few moments as the hum of the engine grows louder. Someone is heading our way.

Who could it be?

Chapter 6

The bright-green Arctic Cat snowmobile races across the lake right to us. The driver slides to a stop in front of us, cuts the engine, and pulls off the green helmet that perfectly matches the sled's hood. We finally discover who it is.

"Hi, Steve," Mom and Dad say together.

"Hey, guys," Steve says. "How's it going?"

"Great!" I respond. "We're doing some ice fishing today."

Steve is a little shorter than my dad and has short brown hair. He is thin and strong but looks larger in his snowmobile clothes. His accent is kind of funny. You can definitely tell he lives in northern Minnesota.

"Looks like you caught dinner," Steve says, looking into our white bucket.

"Yep. The sunfish have been biting like crazy," Dad says.

"How long has your flag been up on your tip-up?" Steve asks with concern.

We all look over at the tip-up. Sure enough, the flag is up!

"No way!" I exclaim.

I jump up and race to the hole, sliding in like a baseball player arriving at home plate. I grab the line and give it a quick pull to set the hook. Instantly, I feel the tug of a fish on the other end.

"Got one!" I yell.

Everyone else hurries over. I start pulling in the line by hand and quickly realize this is not your ordinary fish. She's enormous.

A fish this big is clearly a female—not to mention she must be really old. Bapoe taught me that.

Once the fish realizes she's hooked, the fight is on. She takes off, and the line starts zipping through my gloves. I try to hold tight, but it's no use. She is winning this battle.

I look down at the tip-up and can see the bare spool through the last strands of line.

My concerned eyes meet Dad's. "I'm almost out of line," I say through clenched teeth. I need some advice—and quick. I struggle to hold the line tight.

"That's thirty-pound-test line. It's not going to break. Pull that fish in. You can do it, Luke!" Dad coaches. It's like he's a trainer in the corner of the boxing ring, and I'm the boxer.

"Come on, man! You got this!" Steve cheers.

"Give it all you got, Luke!" Crystal is excited too.

It's me against the fish, and I have a crowd watching. I am not going to let this fish win.

With all my might, I squeeze the line to stop it from slipping through my gloves. I pull and pull, gaining about six inches each time. Then it seems to get easier.

"She must be getting tired. I'm gaining on her," I say.

I keep pulling, now getting a foot at a time. Finally, I see a flash of green under the hole.

"There she is!" I yell. A bead of sweat drips down my nose.

Everyone leans in to look. Crystal and Dad bonk heads and start laughing.

Just when I'm ready to declare myself the winner, the line starts zipping through my fingers again.

"I guess she wasn't done," Steve says. "Those big ones don't like to come through the hole." Clearly, he's speaking from experience.

I clamp down again as hard as I can. My arms are getting tired, and now I'm being pulled closer to the hole.

"Let me know if you need any help," Dad says.

"Thanks, but I got this!"

I don't care how big it is. There is no way I am going to get any help pulling in a fish—especially not in front of Steve.

I grunt and pull back with all my might. After a few moments, I feel a little give. I start gaining on her and pulling in line faster than before. Once again, I see the magical green of a giant northern pike flashing in the hole.

Everyone crowds closer, trying to get a look at this beauty.

I pull hard and see the giant head for a moment.

"It's as big as the hole!" I say with eyes that match my concern.

I collect myself and take in a big breath. I need all my strength to get this giant up onto the ice. Pulling with everything I have, I manage to get her head into the hole. Then, like a massive snake, she slips up onto the ice.

I let out a huge sigh of relief. Everyone starts cheering and smacking me on the back like I'm a rag doll. Crystal jumps up and down like I scored a touchdown or something. This is crazy!

"That's the biggest northern pike I've ever seen caught on this lake," Steve says.

"Thank you." With a proud smile, I let Steve's words sink in. That's pretty cool.

Dad quickly pops the hook out of the giant's mouth. She lies on the ice completely still, clearly tired out.

I carefully slide my gloves under her and lift her up. She is so heavy that I have to hold her against my chest. It doesn't bother me for one second that I'm getting fish slime all over my jacket.

Dad and Mom snap some pictures with their cell phones. No one has to tell me to smile—I'm grinning from ear to ear.

"Look at that right fin," Steve says. "It's half the size of the left one. It must have been bitten off when the fish was younger. It's amazing to think what a fish this old has been through."

"All right," Dad says. "Let's get it back in the hole. We want to keep this fish healthy."

He's right. I want to get her back in the water. It's exciting to know that a fish this big lives in the lake.

Leaning down, I guide her into the hole. She goes headfirst—just like how Crystal and I go down the tube slide at the water park. The fish wiggles her tail the whole way down. That's a good sign. She's happy to get back in the water.

I slowly shake my head in amazement and look at everyone. "Wow! That was cool!"

"You can say that again!" Crystal adds, still beaming a big smile.

"That was a giant! It gets me fired up to get in my dark house!" Steve says. Then he turns to me. "Hey—do you and Crystal want to come with me? Want to try spearing a northern?"

Chapter 7

Crystal and I look at each other, and our jaws drop. Then we turn and stare at Steve's black fish house across the lake. After a few moments, I spin back around to Steve.

"Absolutely!"

"I'm in too!" Crystal adds.

"Come on, then! Hop on your sleds," he says, motioning toward our snowmobiles.

All three of us look to Mom and Dad for approval. They just smile and wave us on.

Crystal and I race to our snowmobiles and follow Steve's Arctic Cat across the lake. We all skid to a stop in front of the house.

Steve walks over, opens the door, and disappears inside the dark interior. I let Crystal follow him inside first. She gets swallowed up by the dark too.

I'm not sure what to expect. I've seen this fish house for so many years but have never been inside. My mind has made up so many stories about the things he might have in here: tackle boxes, a small heater, a lantern, and a bunch of fishing rods stacked up in the corner.

As soon as I walk in, I realize all those stories were wrong.

The walls are painted black, and there are no windows. A wild-looking steel spear is propped up in the corner, along with a four-foot-long chisel. Two little chairs sit next to a big square cutout in the middle of the plywood floor. There is nothing else inside—it's bare.

We can see the ice through the open square cutout. All the snow is removed, and the ice is crystal clear. It's like we're giant hockey fans looking down at a tiny ice rink.

"Please shut the door, Luke," Steve asks.

I pull it shut, and the sunlight gets squeezed out. I latch the door from the inside and then take another look around. Like magic, the whole place glows from the light coming in through the ice.

Steve grabs the black steel chisel. Like an artist, he carefully starts chipping into the ice. He's tracing the outline of the square. He doesn't need a big auger like we used to drill our holes. We used the auger because we were making brand-new holes that had to go through two feet of thick ice. But Steve's been using this same hole in the cutout area all winter. All he has to do is chisel out about two inches of thin ice that has reformed on the top.

Crystal and I back up and give him room as he makes his way around. When he gets back to where he started, he delivers one last knock on the ice.

The whole block of ice breaks loose. With one blow to the middle, he breaks the ice into two perfect, equal pieces. He slides his chisel under the half closest to me and raises it up.

"Grab that, please," he says.

I pick up the big chunk of perfectly clear ice. I'm careful because it's as slippery as an eel.

"Crystal, can you open the door for Luke? Luke, bring that outside and toss it to the side of the house."

Crystal opens the door, and I get blinded by the sun. My eyes have already adjusted to the darkness inside. Squinting, I walk around to the side and toss the ice on top of several other chunks piled in the snow.

Crystal comes right behind me with the other piece. She tosses hers onto the pile, and it cracks apart like breaking glass.

"Whoa," she says, clearly entertained.

We go back inside and latch the door closed behind us. The square cutout now looks like a mini swimming pool—perfectly smooth and glowing from below.

"*Wowww* . . ." Crystal says in total amazement.

"How cool is that?" I say, staring down into the water and slowly shaking my head.

"Amazing!" Crystal agrees.

It's like we're looking down into another world. The ice around the hole is clear, sparkling, and about two feet thick. It looks more like glass than ice.

The clear, glowing water is tinted slightly green from the bottom of the lake. There are five long green weeds suspended motionless about two feet below the ice. The bottom, which seems to be about ten feet down, is brown and green. A twisted nest of dead and living weeds covers the bottom of the lake.

"Do you see those tiny minnows down there?" Crystal asks.

I focus in and notice what she's talking about. There are a few minnows weaving in and out of the weed clumps.

"I see them," I say. "There's a tiny sunfish too."

"This is one of the coolest things I've ever seen," Crystal says. "It's like an aquarium."

"Just wait until I bring some *real* fish in," Steve says.

Crystal and I can barely contain our excitement. We're ready for some action!

Chapter 8

Steve drops the lure into the water. It's attached to a line, which is tied to an eyelet on the wall. I'm sure that's so he doesn't lose the lure to the bottom of the lake if he lets go of the line. The lure is painted green and orange and has small wings on each side, but it doesn't have any hooks. The whole lure is about the length of my hand.

"Looks like a flying fish to me," Crystal says.

"You're right. I never thought of it that way," Steve replies.

Steve stops the lure about four feet down. He begins a slow pattern of pulling it up and then letting it swim down. The fish-like lure starts going in a circle.

Suddenly, a little northern pike about a foot long shoots in and attacks the lure. He doesn't take it, though. He vanishes as quickly as he appears. The lure bounces after the attack.

"Whoa! That was interesting!" Crystal says.

"Just a little guy." Steve's voice is calm, like he's seen this a hundred times. "We want them bigger than that."

Steve keeps working the lure. A minute later, a large northern glides into the opening.

"That's what we're looking for," Steve whispers. "Crystal, grab the spear and give it a shot."

Crystal's eyes get big, and she shakes her head. "No way. Not a chance. You show us how to do it first!"

Smirking, Steve slowly reaches over and grabs the spear with his right hand. With his left hand, he stops moving the lure. It glides to a halt.

The northern slowly closes in on the lure. Then it opens its mouth and bites the head. It spits the lure out, clearly not liking the hard plastic. But the northern doesn't leave.

Steve eases the spear into the water about six inches. "You need to have the spear in the water before you fling it. If not, you'll miss every time. It's a water angle thing," he whispers, teaching us the ropes.

Then, like throwing a dart, he quickly lets it fly. The spear connects right behind the northern pike's head and sticks in.

The fish tries to swim away, but Steve easily pulls it in using the rope attached to the spear. The wiggling fish breaks through the water and lands in Steve's waiting right hand. He pulls the spear out and holds the fish up.

"And that's how it's done! A perfect one for dinner." Steve says proudly. A rare smile fills his face.

We congratulate Steve as he makes his way around us. He knocks the latch open with a free hand and nudges the door open. Then he tosses the fish outside onto the snow. "Now are you ready, Crystal?" Steve asks.

"I'll give it a try," she says.

"Great. You're up!"

Steve starts making the lure dance in circles again. Minutes later, a small northern swims into the opening and pokes at the lure. Steve teases the fish by pulling the lure around faster, but the little guy keeps after it.

Then a bigger northern shoots in and takes a bite at the lure. The small northern takes off quickly, but the bigger one stays put.

"OK, Crystal. Get him," Steve says softly.

Crystal picks up the spear and eases it into the water.

"It's a little heavier than I thought," she whispers.

"That helps it zip through the water. Go a little bit lower," Steve coaches. "Lower. Lower. All right, let him have it!"

Crystal shoves the spear down and lets it go. It flies right past the fish and sticks into the weeds at the bottom.

Steve and I groan like she just missed the winning shot at the buzzer.

"That's OK—you'll get him next time. It takes some practice," Steve says with calm confidence and no judgment.

Crystal pulls the spear up and lets the water drain off.

Moments later, another northern is back, eyeing the lure again. Maybe it's the same one, actually. It's coming in pretty slow, like it's being cautious. I'm sure a flying spear isn't something it sees every day.

Crystal readies the spear and eases it into the water. She slides the prongs down about six inches.

"Perfect. Let it fly when you're ready," Steve whispers.

Crystal takes aim and flicks her wrist. The spear rockets down and connects with the tail of the fish.

Steve and I both cheer. She did it!

The fish tries to swim away, but those prongs are not letting go. Crystal pulls the fish out of the water and onto the floor of the house. It's wiggling like crazy, and Crystal screams.

Like a pro, Steve grabs the fish behind the gills, removes the spear, and has control in a second.

"I got it. Great job, Crystal! You did it!" Steve high-fives Crystal with his free hand.

"Way to go, Crystal. That was awesome!" I add.

Steve heads for the door and tosses the northern outside. It lands next to the first one.

"OK, Luke. You're up," Steve says, closing the door again.

I could not be more excited. I already love spearfishing, and I haven't even tried it yet!

I take the spear and move next to Steve. He's already making the lure swim in circles. I start to ready the spear. But before I even get settled, the same little northern swims up.

"He's definitely persistent," Steve says. "Must be hungry."

The little northern suddenly shoots off, and soon we know why. A giant northern pike glides into the opening, stopping about six inches from the lure. Steve brings the lure to a halt.

"Look at that!" Steve's words come out slow. "It's giant."

The head and tail barely fit into our view through the square cutout. This fish is really wide too!

"Oh my goodness," Crystal gasps.

"Should I take it?" I ask.

Steve's silence indicates he's thinking this through. I look over at him, hoping for a quick answer.

"That's definitely a giant female. I think we should pass on her," he replies.

After a moment, I understand what he means. I'm used to regular fishing, where we use hooks. We can catch a fish and then release it back to the water without killing it. With spearfishing, though, there is no "release." A fish likely won't survive after it's been speared. Whatever you catch becomes your dinner. For a big female like this, then, it's best to let her be."It's crazy, though," Steve says. "In one day, we've found two of the biggest northerns I've ever seen on this lake."

"Wait a minute!" I point down at the fish. "Look at the right fin. It's smaller than the left fin."

"You're right, Luke. That's the *same* northern you caught earlier. How bizarre is that?"

We stand still in amazement and watch her. Steve tries to tease her a little by moving the lure. She doesn't move. She's not going to take the bait. Then, like a silent submarine, she eases away and disappears.

"That was so cool!" Crystal says.

"Yeah, what a fish!" I'm still kind of in shock. "And if I would have kept her earlier, we never would have seen her again like this. Isn't that something?"

Suddenly, another northern about as long as my arm swims into the opening. This must be a hot spot for northern pike—clearly why Steve puts the house here year after year!

"Get ready, Luke. Game on!" Steve says.

I grip the spear, and my heart starts pounding. This is it—my first attempt. I ease the spear into the water, learning from both Steve and Crystal. I wait for the perfect shot, just like when I'm bowhunting.

Then I hear Steve say, "Take him!"

I flick my wrist and let the spear fly. The spear catches the fish right in the middle.

"Boom!" I yell. "I got him!"

"Yes! Good throw, Luke!" Steve says.

I pull that baby up and grab him behind the gills. I pull out the spear and lift the northern high with my right arm.

"Winner, winner, fish dinner!" I say.

We all laugh.

I stare at the northern in my hands and think about all the fish we've caught today. This has turned out to be one of the best fishing adventures yet.

A knock on the door brings us back to reality. Crystal opens the door to find Dad standing there with a big smile on his face.

"Sounds and looks like you guys are having some luck." He is straddling the two northerns already lying on the ice by the door.

"Heads up! Another one is coming out," I say, laughing.

Dad steps to the side, and I toss my northern out onto the snow.

"I'm glad you guys helped Steve put some fish in his freezer. I'm sure he and his family will enjoy them."

"Oh, we will," Steve replies. "These guys are doing great. The fish don't stand a chance."

"That's fantastic," Dad says. "But it's time to head back to the cabin, you two."

"Oh man! But we were just getting started," I plead.

I don't want to leave yet, and Steve senses my disappointment.

"I'll be back tomorrow morning around eight. You guys are welcome to join me," he offers.

Crystal and I both look at Dad for an answer.

"That's fine with me," he says, nodding in approval.

"Yes!" Crystal and I shout. We high-five.

We thank Steve and jump on our snowmobiles for the ride home. We follow Dad and Mom up the hill, past Mr. Boney's old cabin. Then we cruise down the trail, weaving through the forest of snow-covered pine trees, white poplars, and giant old oaks.

I smile under my helmet as I think about the day we've had: snowmobiling, hot dogs over the fire, tons of hard-fighting sunfish, the biggest northern of my life, and spearfishing. Who could ask for more?

I love it up here. I can't wait to see what tomorrow brings!

About the Author

Kevin Lovegreen was born, raised, and lives in Minnesota with his loving wife and two amazing children. Hunting, fishing, and the outdoors have always been a big part of his life. From chasing squirrels as a child to chasing elk as an adult, Kevin loves the thrill of hunting. But even more, he loves telling the stories of the adventure. Presenting at schools and connecting with kids about the outdoors is one of his favorite things to do.

Monster Mule Deer

Lucky Luke's
25lb. turkey

The
Muddy
Elk

Crystal's
1st buck

Lucky Luke
with a large-
mouth bass

Lucky Luke's
1st bear

Crystal, The Swamp hero!

www.KevinLovegreen.com

Other books in the series

To order books or learn about
school visits please go to:
www.KevinLovegreen.com

All the stories in the Lucky Luke's Hunting Adventures series are based on real experiences that happened to me or my family.

If you like the book, please help spread the word by telling all your friends!

Thanks for reading!
Kevin Lovegreen